King Lear

Sweet
Cherry

Published by Sweet Cherry Publishing Limited
Unit 36, Vulcan House,
Vulcan Road,
Leicester, LE5 3EF
United Kingdom

First published in the US in 2013
2020 hardback edition

2 4 6 8 10 9 7 5 3

ISBN: 978-1-78226-727-0

©Macaw Books

King Lear

Based on the original story from William Shakespeare,
adapted by Macaw Books.

Lexile® code numerical measure L = Lexile® 1140L

Guided Reading Level = T

Cover design and illustrations by Macaw Books

www.sweetcherrypublishing.com

Printed and bound in India
I.TP002

About *Shakespeare*

William Shakespeare, regarded as the greatest writer in the English language, was born in Stratford-upon-Avon in Warwickshire, England, in 1564. He was the third of eight children born to John and Mary Shakespeare.

Shakespeare was a poet, playwright and dramatist. He is often known as England's national poet and the "Bard of Avon." Thirty-eight plays, one hundred and fifty-four sonnets, two long narrative poems and several other poems are attributed to him. Shakespeare's plays have been translated into every major existent language and are performed more often than those of any other playwright.

Cordelia: She is the youngest daughter of King Lear. She is disowned by her father when she refuses to flatter him. She marries the King of France. At the end of the play, she comes to help her father and forgives him for all his ill will towards her.

King Lear: He is the King of Britain. He loves power and flattery, and does not like being contradicted. He wants to enjoy the authority of being king, even though he has unburdened himself of a king's responsibilities.

Goneril: She is the eldest daughter of King Lear and the wife of the Duke of Albany. She flatters her father in order to receive one-third of his kingdom. She is jealous, treacherous and ruthless.

Earl of Kent: He is a nobleman and a loyal subject of King Lear. He disguises himself as Caius when King Lear banishes him, so that he can serve his master. He continues to get himself into trouble throughout the play.

King Lear

Once upon a time, England was ruled by an old and wise king called Lear. King Lear had three daughters—the eldest, Goneril, was married to the Duke of Albany; Regan, his

second daughter, was married
to the Duke of Cornwall; and
his youngest daughter was
called Cordelia, for whom the
King of France and the Duke
of Burgundy were suitors.

After his eightieth birthday,
King Lear felt that it was time
for him to resign from the

matters of the state and spend the last few years of his life in other pursuits. So he called for his three daughters, to hear from their own lips how much they loved him. He had decided that according to their declarations, he would divide the kingdom amongst them.

His eldest daughter Goneril had already come to know about his intentions and therefore immediately started proclaiming her love for him in unearthly context. She told him that she loved him more than the light of

her own eyes and that there were no words which could adequately describe her love for him. The king was overjoyed and decided to give her and her husband one-third of his entire kingdom.

After Goneril came Regan. She was one step ahead of her elder sister, and the minute she entered the room and her father asked her how much she loved him, she replied that she loved him much, much more than

Goneril could ever declare. She went on to say that all other joys were dead in comparison to the love that she had for her dear father. Lear was obviously flattered on hearing this, and within an instant he bestowed another third of his kingdom upon her and her husband.

Finally, it was time for Cordelia, his youngest daughter, to enter and declare her love for her father. Now that Lear had already heard his other daughters speak of their love for him, he was sure that Cordelia would love him more

than Goneril and Regan put together. But Cordelia, who had already seen the pretense of her two sisters, merely replied that she loved him as much as she should, no more and no less.

Lear was completely shocked by his daughter's seemingly harsh words, and thinking it was

in jest, he asked her to rethink
lest her fortune be marred. But
Cordelia was adamant. She said
that she loved her father a lot,
honored him and respected him,
but once she was married, she
would have to share her love with
her husband as well. She then
went on to ask why, since both

her sisters had made such tall claims about their love for their father, they had got married at all. Surely they should have stayed with their father!

In reality, Cordelia was

the only daughter who loved
Lear to the heights which her
sisters had expressed. But when
she learned that her sisters had
betrayed their father in order
to acquire his money and that
they did not love him at all,
Cordelia decided that she would

not boast about her love for him,
since she did not care about
his money or his kingdom.

But old age had completely
clouded Lear's sense of reason
and he could not tell the
difference between who loved

him and who did not. He was so
agitated by Cordelia's response
that he immediately withdrew
the third part of the kingdom
he had kept for her and divided
it between Goneril and Regan
and their husbands. He retained
the title of king for himself
and concluded an arrangement

whereby he, along with his one
hundred attendants, would spend
one month in succession at the
castles of his two daughters.

These arrangements seemed
extremely risky to the kingdom,
yet no one had the courage to
defy the king's orders. Only
the Earl of Kent, his most loyal

subject, who cherished him as a father and honored him as his master, spoke up. But this only stirred the king's wrath even more. He was so angry with the Earl of Kent for trying to defend Cordelia that he at once banished him from the court.

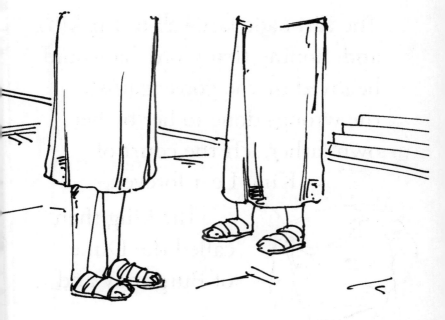

The earl bade farewell to the king
and, hoping that Cordelia would
be saved by the gods against
the wrongs done to her by her
own father, left the court of
King Lear forever.

The king then
called the Duke
of Burgundy and

the King of France to court. He
explained Cordelia's predicament
and how she had come to lose
everything because of her harsh
words. She would now have no
dowry to offer them, and this
information immediately made
the Duke of Burgundy stop
loving Cordelia and he walked off

in a huff, rejecting any further alliance. But the King of France understood what had happened

and said that Cordelia's virtue
and honesty meant much more
to him than any kingdom.
Taking her hand in his, he
asked her to bid farewell to her
sisters and father, and to leave
with him for France, where she
would live as his queen forever.

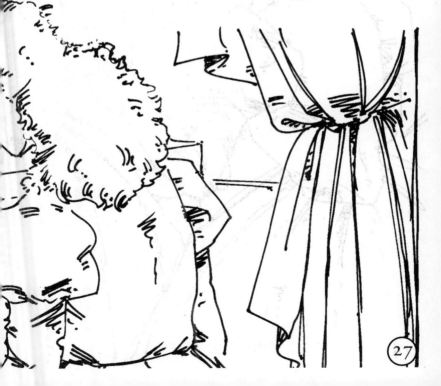

Cordelia wished her sisters well, and asked them to take care of their father and love him as much as they had expressed. The sisters asked her not to preach to them and, after a

tearful farewell, Cordelia left for France with her husband-to-be.

Lear's daughters, Goneril and Regan, began to show their true colors within a few days of Cordelia's departure. Lear first noticed this when he was a guest at the house of Goneril. She would feign sickness or pretend

that she was busy whenever her father tried to talk to her, and generally make a show of her displeasure in being bothered by him. Even the servants started to neglect him and would refuse to obey his orders.

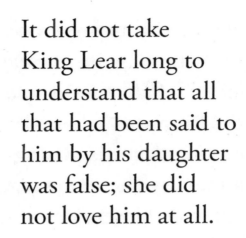

It did not take
King Lear long to
understand that all
that had been said to
him by his daughter
was false; she did
not love him at all.

However, in the
face of such adversity,
there are some who
have always respected
you and cherished
your company, and
who do their duty
once again. Such a
man was the Earl of
Kent. Though Lear
had banished him
and said he would be

executed if he were ever found in Britain again, the earl had not left. He had stayed to ensure that the king was safe and taken care of. So, after disguising himself as a man by the name of Caius, he entered the services of the king,

but not for a second did Lear
realize that the man serving him
was the banished Earl of Kent.

Lear had one supporter
left besides Caius: the royal
jester who had stayed loyal to
the king through all his trials

and tribulations. He had kept
the king entertained and tried
to make him smile when he
had lost all reason to do so.

Finally, Goneril came to her father one day and informed him that he was inconveniencing her by staying at her castle for so long and that she wanted him to leave immediately. As if that were not enough, she also informed him that he should seek company with people who were more his own age and would provide him with better company.

Lear was dumbstruck.

He could not believe that the same Goneril who had showered him with love was now telling him to leave. He immediately ordered his horses to be saddled and decided to leave for Regan's house. He cursed Goneril and wished that she should never have a child, for one day she would

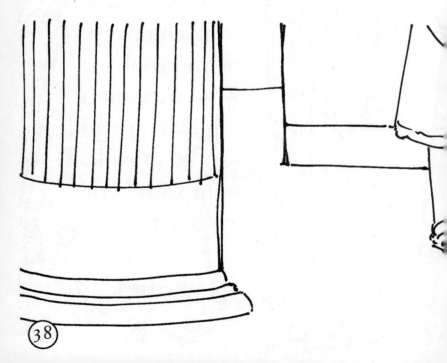

probably even ask the child to leave. Lear left her castle at once.

Lear asked Caius to go on ahead and inform Regan that he was on his way, but it seemed that Goneril had already informed Regan about her father's inconveniencing ways. She had also asked Regan not to

entertain her father's one hundred
attendants, as she claimed
that they were a nuisance.

When Regan came
to know of this,
though Caius was
a messenger of
King Lear, she
had him locked

up. When Lear arrived at the castle, the first thing he saw was his own messenger in chains. Then he discovered to his utter dismay that his daughter and her husband were not even there to receive him. Upon seeing how angry he was, they came out at last, but Lear was heartbroken to see that Goneril was with them. Only now was he starting to see the virtue of Cordelia's words.

Regan, as if in a bid to outdo her sister, declared that the one hundred attendants her father had with him were a bit too much and that only twenty-five should stay. This shocked Lear, as he realized that his

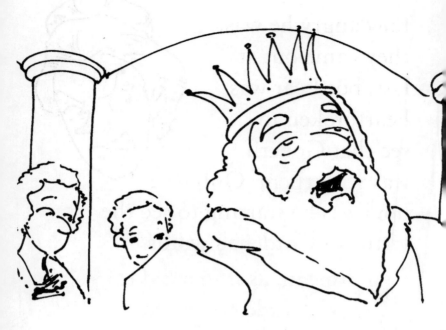

own daughters did not care
about his honor and prestige.
Goneril further commented
that actually he had no need
for any attendants at all.

Lear then decided that under
no circumstances would he enter
either of their castles, and though

a violent storm had begun, he
mounted his horse and set off to
the countryside. Neither of his
daughters tried to stop him.

Even though he took shelter
under a large tree, the poor
king was splattered by the rain.
The jester tried to entreat his
master to return, but Lear was

adamant that he would rather take the evil temperament of nature than beg his daughters to show him any mercy.

Caius, who had been released by Regan's men, found his master and refused to

have him stand there in the storm. He took him to a small hovel, where they could take shelter. There the king saw a beggar, who was lying in the cold with nothing but a blanket over him. Lear remarked to Caius that perhaps he too was a father who had given everything away to his unkind daughters! The poor king seemed to have gone insane.

As the storm subsided, the Earl

49

of Kent, along with the help
of some of the king's faithful
attendants, took Lear to the
Castle of Dover, where he had
friends. Leaving King
Lear there to be
looked after by
his people, the
earl hastened
to France

to meet Cordelia, now the
Queen of France, and inform
her of her father's condition.
The minute she heard what
had happened, she set off for
Dover at once with the royal
French army. She had decided
to subdue her sisters and restore
her father's kingdom to him.

Meanwhile, Lear had managed to escape from the castle and run away to the countryside. He was found by Cordelia's entourage stark raving mad, running around singing with a crown of straw on his head. Cordelia's physicians gave him some medication and soon, father and daughter were

reunited. Lear was overjoyed
to see the daughter who really
loved him and asked for her
forgiveness, but Cordelia said that
he had done nothing to require
her forgiveness in the first place.

Meanwhile, the two evil
sisters were having troubles of

their own. They had both fallen
in love with Edmund, the Earl of
Gloucester, who had
himself cheated
his brother Edgar
out of his rightful
title. At that time,
Regan's husband,

the Duke of Cornwall, died.
Regan immediately decided to
marry Edmund, but this did not
go down well with Goneril, who
also wanted to marry him. She
poisoned Regan to get her out
of the picture, but was caught in

the act. Goneril's husband, the Duke of Albany, also learned of her love for the Earl of Gloucester and put her behind bars. Unable to bear the

humiliation, Goneril took her own life.

During this time, another tragic event was the death of Cordelia. Regan and Goneril had both sent large armies to meet Cordelia's army, under the leadership of the Earl of Gloucester. Cordelia was captured and killed in prison on Edmund's orders. Lear did not live long after she died.

Cordelia had lived a full life, for she had even had the opportunity to serve her dear father one last time and all had been resolved between them.

The Earl of Kent, who was also the faithful Caius, could not cope with his master's death. Like the true faithful servant, he followed him to his

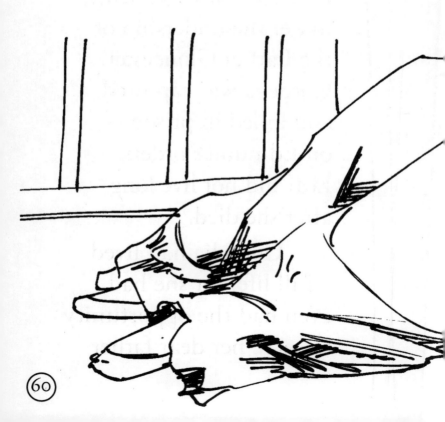

grave, perhaps to take care of
his noble master in heaven.

The saga ended when the
evil Edmund, the wrongful
Earl of Gloucester, was killed in

battle with his brother Edgar,
the rightful earl. Goneril's
husband, the Duke of Albany,
who had always been averse to
his wife's treatment of her father,

ascended the throne of Britain.
He ruled wisely for many years.